The Frog Prince

One fine evening, a beautiful Princess went out for a walk in the woods. After walking for some time, she felt tired and decided to rest near a spring of cool water. The Princess had brought along her favourite plaything, a golden ball to play with.

A little later, the Princess started playing with her golden ball near the spring. She tossed the ball so high that it fell into the spring. "Oh! If only I could get back my golden ball, I would give away all the jewels that I have," she cried out.

While the Princess sat crying, a frog jumped out of the water and asked, "Why are you crying, Princess ? The Princess looked up at the frog and said, "My golden ball has fallen into the spring and I want it back. But why are you asking? You can't help me, ugly frog."

"I can fetch your ball, Princess. In return you must take me with you, allow me to eat out of your golden plate and sleep in your bed," croaked the ugly frog. The Princess thought, 'This frog will never reach the palace but he can certainly fetch my golden ball for me.'

"I will do as you say but first you must fetch my ball for me," said the Princess. The frog jumped into the water at once and returned with the golden ball. "Ah! You found it," cried the Princess, with joy and took the golden ball from him.

The next moment, the Princess began running towards the palace ignoring her promise to the ugly frog, but the frog kept on crying out to her, "Take me with you, Princess." The Princess did not pay heed to his cries and ran on.

The next day, when the Princess sat down to dine, she heard a loud knock on the door. A voice called out, "Open the door, Princess. Do you remember the promise you made by the spring in the woods?" The Princess opened the door and, to her dismay found the ugly frog sitting at the threshold.

The Princess was surprised. She had not expected the frog to reach her palace. She banged the door on the frog's face. When she was returning to the dining table, the King noticed that the princess was frightened. He asked, "What is the matter? Why are you so disturbed, dear?" The Princess told her father all that had happened in the woods. At that very moment there was another loud knock on the door.

The King said, "Princess, you must keep your word. Let him in." Unwillingly, the Princess opened the door and the frog quickly hopped inside. When the ugly frog came close to the table, he said, "Dear Princess, please lift me up and put me on the table so that I can eat from your plate."

The poor Princess had no choice but to agree. The frog ate from the Princess' plate. When he had eaten to his heart's content, he said, "I am tired. Please, carry me to your bed." Again the Princess had to agree to the frog's instruction. She took the frog to her room and put him on her pillow, where he slept all night long.

With the first rays of the
sun, the frog woke up and
hopped out of the Princess' room.
When the Princess saw him leave, she
thought, "At last, my troubles will be over. That ugly
frog is going away!" The Princess was proved wrong
for as soon as it was evening, the frog returned to the
palace.

Once again, the frog ate with the Princess and slept on her bed. Again, the next morning with the first rays of the sun, he hopped out of the palace. Things went on in the same manner on the third evening as well. "How will I ever get rid of this ugly frog?" said the Princess to herself.

When the Princess woke up the next morning, she was astonished to see a handsome Prince standing beside her bed, gazing down at her. "Who are you?" asked the Princess. "I am the ugly frog," replied the handsome Prince.

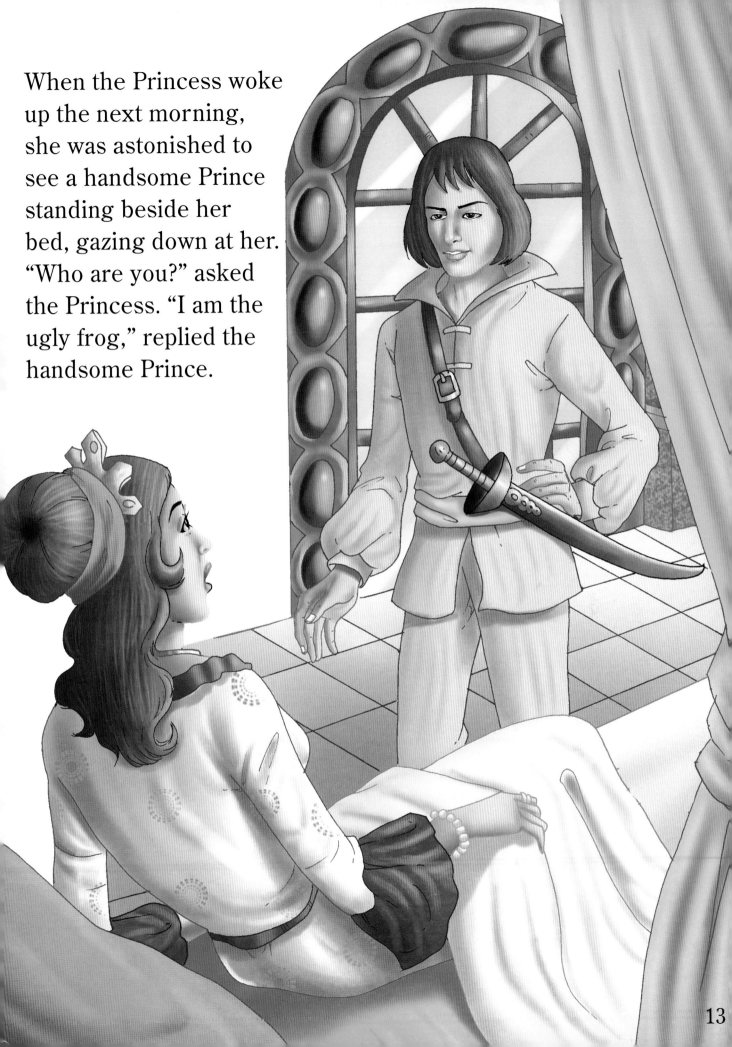

"I was cursed by an evil fairy. She had turned me into a frog. Her spell could only be broken when a Princess allowed me to eat from her plate and sleep on her bed for three nights," the Prince continued.

14

"You, my beautiful Princess, have broken the charm. You kept your promise and allowed me to stay with you for three evenings. I can only thank you by asking you to marry me," he said. The Princess was delighted at this proposal and agreed to marry the Prince.

The King was surprised to hear the tale of the handsome Prince and readily gave his consent for the wedding. The wedding was celebrated with great splendour. A few days later, the Prince returned to his Kingdom with his newly wedded wife, where they lived happily ever after.